Least of All

Least of All

Carol Purdy

illustrated by Tim Arnold

Margaret K. McElderry Books
NEW YORK

Library of Congress Cataloging-in-Publication Data

Purdy, Carol.
Least of all.

Summary: A little girl in a big farm family teaches
herself to read using the Bible and shares this knowledge
with her brothers, parents, and grandmother during a
long, cold Vermont winter.
[1. Farm life—Fiction.   2. Reading—Fiction]
I. Arnold, Tim, ill.   II. Title.
PZ7.P9745Le   1987   [E]   86-12613
ISBN 0-689-50404-7

Margaret K. McElderry Books
Macmillan Publishing Company
866 Third Avenue
New York, N.Y. 10022
Collier Macmillan Canada, Inc.

Composition by Boro Typographers, Inc.
New York, New York
Printed and bound in Hong Kong by Toppan Printing Co.

10   9   8   7   6   5   4   3   2   1
First Edition

To Michael, Laura, Mark and Sarah

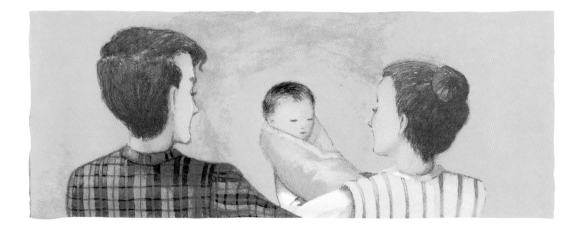

Most of all was Papa and Mama. Then Grandmama and the brothers: Joshua, Malachi, Samuel, Aaron and Ezekiel. Least of all was Raven Hannah.

When Papa had first seen his baby daughter's thick hair he said, "Her hair is black as a raven. Let's call her Raven."

"But the boys' names are all from the Bible," said Grandmama. "Why don't you call her Hannah?"

"Raven is from the Bible," said Papa. "Remember Noah's ark and the raven?"

"Of course," said Mama. "Let's name her Raven Hannah."

Papa always let Aaron or Ezekiel drive to church so they could learn to handle the horses like the older boys. Every Sunday Raven Hannah asked, "Can I hold the reins on the way home?"

And every Sunday Papa said, "You're not big enough."
In those days there was not much a little sister could do on a Vermont farm. But there was work aplenty for Mama, Papa, Grandmama and five strong boys.

In autumn Joshua cut firewood with Papa. Malachi and Samuel hauled it from the woodlot. Now that Raven Hannah was six years old, Malachi let her ride on the jostling pile of logs. She loved the smell of fresh-sawed wood and the boys' shouts echoing in the keen, cold air.

Aaron split the logs for Mama's cookstove and left some larger ones for the fireplaces. Ezekiel stacked the wood along the covered passage between house and barn.

Sometimes Raven Hannah carried a small splintery piece. But Ezekiel was faster, and she got in his way.

When maple sugaring season came at the end of winter, Raven Hannah ran here and there in the crunchy snow, first pestering Ezekiel and Aaron for an icy sip of sweet sap from their buckets...

...then flitting to the sugar shack to watch the great roaring fire beneath a cauldron of bubbling syrup. She felt the flames glow on her face and breathed maple steam until Joshua told her she was a nuisance and shooed her out into the cold.

Soon her toes began to feel numb, so Raven Hannah went
to see what mischief she could make for Samuel and Malachi
as they pitched hay to the winter-bound cows.

"I'll tell Papa," Samuel warned.

When snow melted in the season Mama called "mud," the cows came fresh, and the boys helped Papa haul pails of warm milk to feed bawling calves. The pails were too heavy for Raven Hannah to carry without slopping on her dress. "Better let the boys do it," Papa said.

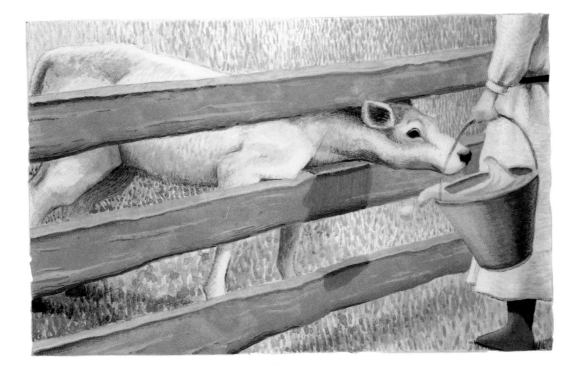

At milking time Raven Hannah nestled in hay still fresh with last summer's scents, cuddling one of Jezebel's new kittens. She watched shafts of milk zing into foaming pails, longing for her hands to grow big enough to help.

Mama and Grandmama transformed the spring rush of milk into smooth wheels of cheese. Once Mama let Raven Hannah pack salted curd into cheese hoops. She carefully filled every crack with the quivering cubes of curd. When Malachi saw her working he teased, "Why the girl is good for something after all."

Raven Hannah glared at him and popped a curd in her mouth. Grandmama didn't notice Malachi's teasing, but she caught Raven Hannah's angry glance and said, "The Lord hateth a proud look and a haughty eye."

With summer's sweet warmth came work to coax rows of corn from the moist, velvety earth of Papa's fields. There was a vegetable garden to hoe and weed and fragrant grasses to cut, rake and stack. Mama, Papa, Grandmama and the boys were busy outside all day.

Now that the cows were on pasture with fresh clover, their cream churned into butter as golden as the daffodils that had bloomed in Grandmama's flowerbed in the spring. Raven Hannah begged to try to churn, and to everyone's surprise, she was big enough at last to take over this important work.

Mama's smile warmed Raven Hannah as she said, "Why of course our girl can churn. She's near seven years old."

But how lonesome Raven Hannah felt as she sat in the cool, musty cellar, plunging a dasher through heavy cream and watching for the first grains of butter.

One day she brought the Bible from the parlor and settled to churning with it open on her lap. To pass time more quickly, she looked at the marks printed on the first page and tried to match them to lines she had memorized at Sunday school when her teacher had spoken them. "In the beginning God created the heaven and the earth. And the earth was without form, and void; and darkness was upon the face of the deep."

She pointed at each word the way she had watched her Sunday School teacher do and even tried to make her voice low and smooth like Mrs. Taylor's.

As Raven Hannah spent her hours at the churn, moving a finger along and reciting words she knew by heart, a wonderful thing happened.

Soon she recognized that many of the marks printed on the page were the same. Then she discovered which word was "God." In a short time "heaven," "earth" and "day" were like old friends.

Before the corn in the fields tasseled, she could read every word in the first chapter. By the time maple leaves again blazed in their full glory of autumn colors, Raven Hannah could find in the Bible the stories of Noah and the ark, Moses in the bulrushes and Daniel in the lion's den.

Her favorite was when Noah sent the raven from the ark—
a bird so strong he flew round and round until the flood waters
dried up from the face of the earth.

She read that story many times and wished mightily that
she were strong—as strong as the raven of the Bible.

Summer and autumn passed. One cold, gloomy afternoon winter's first snowstorm came. The time was right, for now the corn was safe in the silo, the hay in the barn loft. The woodpile was big enough to last through till spring. Juicy carrots and turnips were stored in the freshly scrubbed cellar beside barrels of apples, jugs of sweet cider, bins of potatoes and tubs of Raven Hannah's beautiful golden butter.

Papa, Mama, Grandmama and the boys shut the cows in the barn. Raven Hannah watched from the window and knew there would be no more churning this year.

After a great stomping of boots and slapping of mittens, the family gathered near the warmth of the cookstove and stared at Raven Hannah.

"What are you doing?" Mama finally asked.

Raven Hannah looked up. "Reading about baby Jesus."

Mama's face paled. "Let's hear," she said softly.

Raven Hannah found the place with her finger. "For unto you is born this day in the city of David a Savior, which is Christ the Lord."

Grandmama gasped, and the boys gaped. Papa slapped his knee. "Who taught you to read?" he sputtered.

Raven Hannah glanced at Mama and saw her big smile coming. "I learned while I was churning. I moved my finger along the marks like Mrs. Taylor does until I knew what words they were."

Grandmama took out her handkerchief.

"Time for chores," Papa said in a husky voice. He and the boys went back out the passage toward the barn as Grandmama slipped into the parlor.

After giving Raven Hannah a hug, Mama went down to the cellar to fetch things for supper, leaving Raven Hannah alone with the quiet of the storm.

Raven Hannah followed Grandmama into the parlor and found she was still using her handkerchief. "What's wrong?" asked Raven Hannah.

"I'm joyed you've learned to read," said Grandmama. "None of us ever had opportunity."

Raven Hannah fingered the limp edges of the Bible and realized it was true. Although the Bible was often quoted and always lay on the parlor table, she had never seen any of the family read it.

Raven Hannah spread her arms and began to skip about the room. A little song danced in her heart, and when she noticed Grandmama's beaming face, she sang it aloud.

"I'm not very big.

I'm not very strong.

But I can do what the boys can't do.

Nor Mama,

Nor Papa,

Nor you."

Grandmama caught Raven Hannah's arm and snuggled her onto her lap. "People can be strong in differing ways," she said. "By learning to read the good book you have proved yourself strong in mind and spirit."

Raven Hannah took Grandmama's hand, calloused by summer's work. "Grandmama, you so love the Bible. I will teach you to read it."

"Do you think you could?" asked Grandmama.

"I know I can," said Raven Hannah. "I will teach you to read the way I learned. And I'm going to teach Joshua and Malachi and Samuel and Aaron and Ezekiel. I will even teach Mama and Papa."

And during the long, cold Vermont winter, that is exactly what Raven Hannah did.

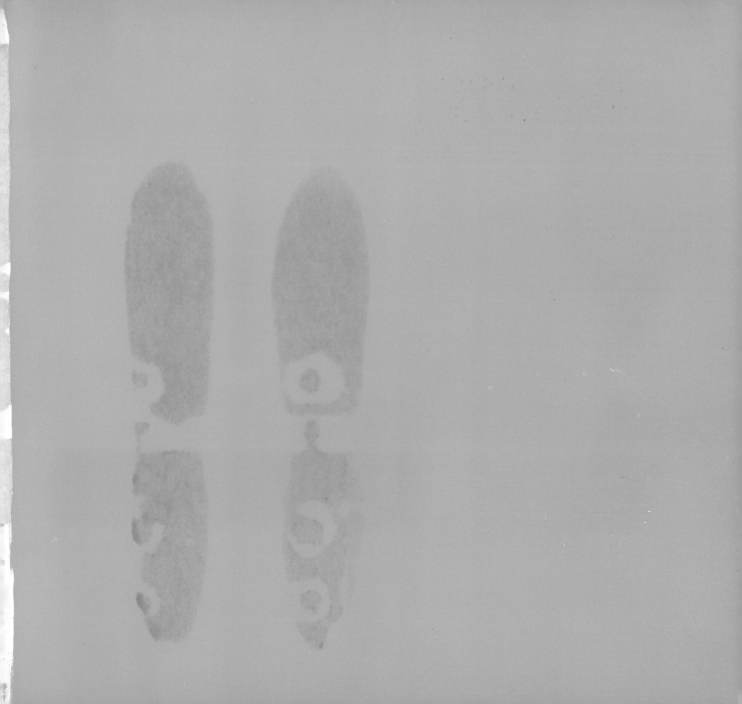